NOBODY'S KING

By **Steven H. West**

Illustrated by **Loraine Potter**

PageWorthy Books

Saint Paul, Minnesota

NOBODY'S KING

By **Steven H. West**
Illustrations by **Loraine Potter**

Published by:
PageWorthy Books
P.O. Box 600095
St.Paul, MN 55106

ISBN 0-9652042-1-9

Library of Congress Catalog Card
Number: 96-92263

Manufactured in the USA
10 9 8 7 6 5 4 3 2 1

DEDICATION

I dedicate this book to all people everywhere, who have ever felt like a nobody. S.W.

SPECIAL ACKNOWLEDGEMENT

A special "thank you!" to Gwen Finke, a now retired third grade teacher, who encouraged the publishing of

NOBODY'S KING.

THE VALLEY

It was an ordinary kind of day in the Valley of Anyplace. A gentle breeze moved slowly through the branches of the large weeping willow trees, causing the leaves to flow back and forth like tidewaters on an ocean beach. Milky-white clouds blanketed the sky and shielded the sun's rays from baking the ground below. Little red squirrels scurried through the tall grass as they took turns chasing each other in a game of tag. Running and chattering, they played tirelessly throughout the morning.

A few birds were chirping their merry little tunes as they flitted from branch to branch in the willow trees.

The bubbling of a nearby stream flowing over and around and between smooth protruding stones, added a sense of peacefulness to the already tranquil picture that the brush of Nature had painted in the Valley of Anyplace.

Off in the distance, this serenity of Nature was broken by the sound of children's voices. When the wind was blowing just right, and one would take the time to stop and listen, many different voices could be heard. There were sounds of laughing, sounds of crying, the voices of boys and the voices of girls. The distant sounds revealed the voices of children of every age. Some were young and some were old, but it seemed that most were somewhere in between.

"Ready-or-not-here-I-come!" was very often heard.

"Stop that! I said, stop that!" was another familiar sound.

"Where's my ball?"

"I had it first!"

"William hit me!"

"Aw, be quiet!"

"William, go to your room!" shouted a much older voice.

"I don't have to!" a voice came back.

"William, go to your room!" said the older voice more sternly.

"I don't want to!" came the reply.

"William, I told you to go to your room, and that's final!"

"Oh, all right."

THE ORPHANAGE

These shouts and cries and complaints and a multitude of other voices could be heard at any time of any day in the Valley of Anyplace.

The sounds were coming from the age-old Anyplace Orphanage. It was odd; it seemed that no matter whose voice was heard, or what was being said, a hidden message could always be understood. It was the same time after time. A child would speak, or laugh, or cry, and somehow two questions could always be heard: "Why doesn't anybody want me?" and "Doesn't somebody love me?"

Oh, these questions were seldom ever asked, but somehow the silent aching hearts of the children could be clearly understood; and every time the still, small voice of Nature would whisper, *"Somebody does!"*

The Anyplace Orphanage was quite a nice place for unwanted children— a home for the homeless. However, it wasn't a very happy place, although it tried so hard to be. Oh, there were toys and games and laughter, but no real happiness — no joy inside. Runaways, children without parents, children whose families didn't want them, these were the children who were at the Anyplace Orphanage.

Children would come and children would go. It was a very busy place. Not only was the orphanage a place where the unwanted were brought to be cared for, it was a place where one would go if a person wanted to adopt a child.

Eventually everyone would leave to go to a new home. Every child dreamed of being part of a family where they would be made to feel special, really be wanted, and truly be loved. For some this dream came true.

But many—far too many—were not so fortunate. Some would come to the orphanage simply looking for a good, strong worker.

All they wanted was some cheap help to work on the farm, or in the coal mine, or loading delivery wagons. In return, the child would get a warm bed, clean clothes, and food to eat. That was all: no love, no affection, and still no joy inside.

"Well," some would say, "at least it's better than the Anyplace Orphanage!"

But was it?

NOBODY

One day a small boy was brought to the orphanage. It was not known where he was from, who his parents were, or even what his name was. In fact, the other children and even the directors of the orphanage didn't seem to care. This boy was so small and frail, and he appeared to be much older than his size would indicate. A rough life often does that to a person's face.

His was not a pleasant face to look at. Scars from the past marred his appearance to the point where people would turn away the moment they would glance at him. He was

not to blame for those scars, though he was treated like each and every one was his own fault. His arms, legs, and entire body bore those terrible scars. He never said where or how he got those horrible marks, but everyone just seemed to know. A lame leg caused him to walk with a limp. His eyesight was weak, and most could see that he was not very smart. This boy always seemed to be dirty: his face, his hands, and his clothes. He wasn't a bad boy. In fact, he never got into any kind of trouble at the orphanage. He would just sit alone with tears in his eyes and watch the other children run and play.

Rarely did the others talk to him, and never did they invite him to join them in their games.

He was nothing that anyone would want: a real nobody. So, because he had no name, and they needed to call him something, they began to refer to him by a name that seemed to fit him perfectly. They simply called him — Nobody.

Visitors and potential parents would come to the orphanage. They would often ask about the poor little scarred boy that was sitting all alone. Others from the orphanage would just look away and say, "Oh, that's Nobody!" Noticed by most, yet wanted by no one, nobody wanted Nobody.

THE MESSAGE

S ome time later, as everyone was gathered for supper, a messenger came to the Anyplace Orphanage. He was an odd kind of fellow, crudely dressed and rough-spoken.

He claimed to be from the Royal Kingdom. From his appearance one could not tell that he was a messenger from the king, but the letter he delivered shattered any trace of doubt.

The letter—the message he brought—was definitely from the king. The letter was stamped with the king's own royal seal. It was like nothing the people at the orphanage had ever seen. The seal, which was of pure gold, bore the monogram -*J.C.*- the initials of the great king.

An air of excitement breezed through the children's home as one of the directors, with trembling hands, began to break the golden seal.

With the seal broken and the letter opened, the contents of the message were revealed.

His Highness, the Royal King, to the directors and children of the Anyplace Orphanage.

Greetings of the warmest kind!

Be it known to you this day, that I, the King, will come to the Anyplace Orphanage one week from today. Precisely at 3:00 P.M. my royal carriage will arrive. I am not sending an ambassador or a spokesman for this visit. I am coming in person!

My purpose will be to seek out one or more children who will return with me to my kingdom. The decision as to which of the children will come with me will be my choice alone. The only condition is that the child agrees to come with me.

Be it understood, the one of my choosing will be brought to my kingdom and be given a new life: one of love, warmth, caring and understanding. This one I will adopt to be my very own child. All of the privileges and responsibilities of my kingdom will be bestowed upon this one I choose.

The old life of this child will not be remembered by anyone in my kingdom. It is the new life they will see. Through my sovereign act of adoption, this one of my choosing will be said to have royal blood.

Remember, my royal carriage will arrive precisely at 3:00 P.M., one week from today. It is expected that you will prepare and be ready for my arrival.

Majestically yours,
J.C., the King

Being certain that the message
was read, and after a few words of
instruction, the king's messenger
turned and left the orphanage.

THE PREPARATION

The level of emotion was high at the Anyplace Orphanage. At first there was great excitement. That excitement soon became mixed with reverent fear. The thought—just the thought—of the king coming for a visit brought an awesome feeling to those at the orphanage.

The week before the scheduled arrival time of the king was a busy one. Everything had to be in order. Three teams were appointed to help with the preparation.

Team number one worked inside
the orphanage. This team's job
was to clean, polish, straighten, and
repair everything inside the home.

The second team was in charge of painting the outside of the orphanage. Wherever the old paint was chipped or scratched or too dirty to wash clean, team number two would paint it.

Team number three did all the
yard work. Cutting grass, trimming
trees and bushes, weeding the garden,
and planting flowers was all done by
this third team.

Little Nobody was excited about the coming of the king and wanted to do what he could to help. But, because everything had to be just right— just perfect for the king— he was told by everyone not to help. He might make a big mistake and ruin everything.

So he was told by everyone to, **"Just stay out of the way!"**

Nobody felt so bad. He just
went to his room and cried. He
thought, "There must be something
I can do for the king."

Just then he got an idea. He
realized that no one had made a
welcome sign for the king. That's
what he would do! He would make
a welcome sign for the king and
put it on a tree by the road so the
king could not miss seeing it. But
he would have to do it secretly;
he could tell no one.

They would never allow it if it were done by little Nobody.

The morning of the king's coming arrived. Last minute preparations were being made by all at the orphanage. The whole place looked very beautiful. One might say it was "fit-for-a-king." The children were all getting ready now. They all bathed, put on clean clothes, and combed their hair. They were all as "neat as pins," and with three hours to spare before the king's carriage was to arrive.

However, Nobody was just finishing up his sign. He had a hard time coming up with the right materials with which to make the sign. The best thing he could find to use without getting into trouble, was an old chalkboard and a few small pieces of chalk. He took his time and did the very best job he could. After all, this sign was for the king.

The sign was now done. Quickly, when no one was looking, he carried the sign down the road and found a tree standing by itself right where the king would be sure to see it. There he nailed the wooden framed welcome sign.

He was so proud of his sign. He did something all by himself—just for the king. He stood back a few steps and smiled to himself as he read the sign:

"WALKOM GRAT KENG."

He did not realize that he had misspelled every word. All he knew was that he had done something special for the king.

Nobody headed back to the orphanage to get ready for the king's coming. Oh, he knew he would never be chosen by the king, but he wanted to look nice anyway.

What a thrill it would be for
Nobody to just be able to see the
king in person. Nobody washed his
face and hands, brushed the dust
off his tattered clothes, and waited for the king to arrive. While he
was sitting all alone, he took a small
piece of paper and a pencil, and
wrote out the same words that he had
put on the sign. He then pinned the
paper to his shirt:

THE VISITOR

It was now shortly after two o'clock. Everyone was quiet, just waiting; when suddenly, the silence was broken by the creaking of the front door. Everyone in the place looked up as a little man walked in. His coat was patched and torn and dusty. His shoes did not match and were extremely worn.

"Just a tramp," everyone thought. The orphanage had seen many of them.

One of the orphanage directors asked rudely, "What do you want?"

"I'm here to adopt a child," came the cheerful reply.

"We can't help you now! Come back tomorrow!" the director said.

"But sir," the little man explained, "I have traveled many miles so I could adopt a child today. I cannot delay another day. I will not leave here without having adopted a child."

"Look mister," said the orphanage director firmly, "the king is coming here in less than one hour. We cannot have you here when he arrives. You're not fit for royalty. We don't want you here!"

The little man bargained, "I'll tell you what. If you let me select a child today, I will quickly make my choice and be gone before the king's carriage arrives."

The director agreed to that just to get him out of the home as soon as possible.

The man began to talk to the children. Few would even acknowledge the man's presence. Those who did were only trying to be polite. None of the children, however, wanted to be adopted by the little man and give up a possible chance of becoming a child of the king.

Then the dusty little man noticed a small boy sitting by himself. As he walked closer to the boy he spotted the little piece of paper that was pinned to his shirt. As he read the paper, he smiled, and then asked, "What's your name, son?"

"That's Nobody!" interrupted a voice from somewhere behind.

Then the man asked, "Did you make that sign down by the road?"

After a somewhat fearful pause, the boy nodded that he did.

"Ah, mighty fine sign, son. Mighty fine sign indeed!" the man replied.

"How would you like to come with me?" the man asked. "I'll feed you, give you a place to stay, and protect you from all that would harm you. I will adopt you and be your father. Not only will we be father and son, but we will be best of friends. What do you say? Will you come with me?"

Nobody thought it over. This was the first person to ever express love to him. He so much wanted to be adopted by someone who would really care for him. He knew the coming king would never adopt him, but he would still like to get just a glimpse of royalty.

After thinking it over, Nobody decided that it was more important that he go with the dusty little man than to see the king. He looked at the man and nodded that he would like to be adopted by him.

In the distance a trumpet sounded, announcing that the king's carriage was very near.

The orphanage director said anxiously, "Here's a paper to sign that says you agree to take good care of this boy, Nobody. Quickly! Sign it and get out of here before the king arrives! We don't want the king to see either of you!"

The trumpet sounded again.

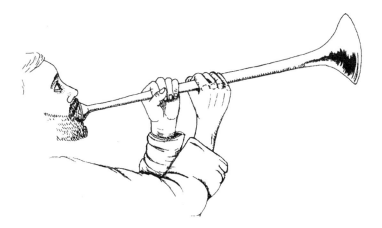

This time the carriage was so close that the horses could be heard trotting up to the home.

"Hurry up, mister! Just sign it and leave out the backdoor—and don't let the king see you!"

As the man signed the paper, the king's carriage stopped in front of the orphanage. The director hurried Nobody and the man out the back door. The time had come to meet the king.

THE ARRIVAL

Once the new father and son were outside, the director went back inside. Hurriedly, he gathered everyone together and they all went out to meet the king.

The carriage was a magnificent sight to behold. The trim of pure gold, polished to a glass-like shine, glowed like fire in the sunlight. Diamonds, rubies, emeralds and sapphires adorned the whole carriage. Four pure white horses pulled the royal coach.

Each horse looked like the others, with mane and tail braided and decorated with silver and gold. Each appeared to be a statue carved out of marble as they stood ever so still.

All from the orphanage stood motion-less—afraid to move—waiting to see the king. No one dared to move. Hearts pounded rapidly as they waited for the king to appear.

Suddenly, the stillness of the moment was broken, not by movement from the carriage, but from near the corner of the orphanage. No one had noticed, but the little man and Nobody had made their way around the side of the home to the front. Everyone looked at the two with embarrassment, frustration and anger.

Just then, every head turned back towards the carriage as the jeweled door swung open.

From the king's carriage stepped a
handsome young man dressed in the
finest clothes that anyone had ever
seen. His pure white robe was so
bright that it nearly blinded the eyes
of the awestruck onlookers.

"Surely, this must be the great king," everyone thought.

But was it? In his right hand he was holding a crown. What a crown it was—pure gold, inlaid with diamonds and rubies. Over his left arm was draped a deep purple robe with threads of gold woven into the fabric.

"That crown and robe," whispered one child to another, *"must be for the one the king will adopt."*

Then what happened shocked all from the orphanage. They could not believe what they saw. The little man —the tramp—and Nobody began to walk toward the royal carriage.

"How disrespectful," they all thought, "to approach the king in that manner."

But no one moved. They just watched.

Now the two were standing in front of the young man who was dressed in white. "Why don't the royal guards do something?" everyone wondered.

As they watched, the little man removed his patched and tattered coat and let it fall to the ground. The young man in white reached out and placed the beautiful crown on the man's head. Then he held the royal robe as the little man carefully and gracefully put it on. The mismatched, worn shoes were kicked off as the king stepped into new shoes that were made of the finest leather.

Yes! This one who came in the
appearance of a tramp was actually
the long awaited king, but he was
despised and rejected by all but one at
the orphanage. The king had come

to them, just as he said he would, but they turned him away.

The king reached into the carriage and pulled out a crown. It was just like his, only smaller. This he placed on the head of little Nobody. After all, Nobody was now a child of the king—he was royalty!

Again the king reached into the carriage. This time he had a beautiful pair of shoes in one hand and in the other a stunning white robe. The king placed the shoes on the ground, and Nobody stepped into them—a perfect fit! Then as the king held the robe for his son, Nobody carefully put it on. Again, a perfect fit! Being adopted by the king meant that

Nobody was indeed a prince—a real prince! All had to agree that little Nobody sure looked like a prince should look. One could not look more princely than Nobody did.

As the children and directors of the Anyplace Orphanage looked on, the king turned and delivered his final message to them.

"One week ago," the king began, "my messenger informed you that I would come to you today. He told you my purpose for coming. He warned you to be prepared and ready. When I arrived today, I was met with behavior that would be unfit treatment for any human being. I did not come as you expected I would.

That is why you were warned to be ready.

"You children, I tried talking to you, but you would not listen. Those who did listen did not hear. You were looking for the great king, and he was right there with you!

"Only one of you agreed to come with me and be adopted by me. This one you have called Nobody, he is now my son. He listened to me and heard me. Today he wears a robe and a crown that only one of great royalty can wear. There is a great feast awaiting him in my kingdom; the celebration has already begun. Truly this is a day of rejoicing for my kingdom.

"All of this could have been yours, but you rejected me. Yes, you laughed at him and made fun of him and called him a Nobody. But now he is mine. He is now a Somebody—Somebody Special!

"I will come by this way again someday. The next time I do, I hope you will all be ready."

With that, the king and his new son entered the beautiful carriage and returned to the royal kingdom, until the day when he would come again and fulfill his promise to return.

(...to be continued!)

ORDER FORM

Additional copies of **NOBODY'S KING**
may be ordered by sending check or money
order for **$8.00** each (price includes first-
class postage and handling) to:

PageWorthy Books
P.O. Box 600095
St. Paul, MN 55106

Please send _____copies of
NOBODY'S KING at $8.00 each to:

Name_____

Addres_____

City_____ State___ Zip_____

_____ I would like to receive information
about future releases from PageWorthy
Books. Please put me on your mailing list.

Comments _____

_____

_____

_____